OLD ONE'S WRATH

CONNOR WHITELEY

No part of this book may be reproduced in any form or by any electronic or mechanical means. Including information storage, and retrieval systems, without written permission from the author except for the use of brief quotations in a book review.

This book is NOT legal, professional, medical, financial or any type of official advice.

Any questions about the book, rights licensing, or to contact the author, please email connorwhiteley@connorwhiteley.net

Copyright © 2021 CONNOR WHITELEY

All rights reserved.

DEDICATION
Thank you to all my readers without you I couldn't do what I love.

OLD ONE'S WRATH

"Brace!" Katrina roared.

Fear gripped them both.

Immediately, herself and her friend; Locke; grabbed on hard to the seats of their shuttle.

As the shuttle entered the large ancient hangar of an even older spaceship, it spun, crashed and bumped along the hangar deck.

Dashing out, Katrina and Locke surged into the hangar as their shuttle was engulfed in burning cleansing flames.

Checking herself, Katrina checked her thick body armour to see that it was intact. Despite the odd bullet hole, laser burn and blade cut.

Relief filled her.

Raising her head, Katrina saw the hangar for the full majesty that it was.

For the hangar was carved from solid black marble with beautiful golden veins pulsing through it.

Katrina as well as Locke were like ants compared to the hangar.

You could easily fit a few fleets of modern battleships in the size of this ancient human hangar.

Snapping her head around, she saw Locke's long black hair that matched his dark skin as well as his chiselled symmetrical face.

He nodded at her.

Stepping forward, Katrina's skin was covered in small speckles of ice and her breath created grand columns in front of her.

She rubbed her hands together.

"What's wrong with the enviro-systems?" Locke asked in a brutish tone.

"I don't know. Do I look like a Techmarine?"

"No, but you studied on Jupiter for a year,"

"One year is nothing. Techmarines go to Jupiter for over a century to learn about technology," Katrina returned.

Kneeling down, she touched the black marbled floor with its golden veins sparkling in the fire of their shuttle.

The crackling roar of the burning shuttle was surprisingly peaceful to Katrina.

She gave a slight smile at the memories evoked by the sound. As she remembered the burning cities and enemies she and Locke had burned over the decades.

Touching the floor, her fingers hummed with electrical energy and the floor looked smooth. Yet her fingers could feel immense lumps and bumps. Like sandpaper.

She breathed in deeply.

Smelling nothing except the artificial air generated by the spaceship with a slight musty smell.

"You're right, Locke. The enviro-systems are broken or something. Smell the Must,"

He nodded. Admiring the vast void of space

outside.

Katrina wondered over to him.

Staring out into the void, they both witnessed immense chunks of decimated ship as well as battleships floating around.

Beyond this ancient battlefield, the bright stars, millions of miles away, reminded the two mercenaries that they needed to escape and return to the Empire.

Katrina flicked freezing cold icy particles off her skin.

"We really screwed up this time didn't we, Locke?"

He gave a brief chuckle.

"That's putting it kindly. We assassinated a Planetary Governor! A Head of State!"

"Well yes, Locke. But we didn't know that at the time,"

"Do you think the Empire cares about that fact? Do you think the Emperor back on Earth will forgive us? Hell, do you think the Empire will ever hire us again?"

Katrina sank a little.

Locke placed a hand on her shoulder.

"We'll be fine. We managed to escape the Hunters before,"

"Ha, the Hunters. The All-Powerful Officers that have complete Authority in the Empire. It was fun escaping them and making it to the Emperor. But this time it's different,"

Locke withdrew the hand and backed away.

"What did you do?"

Katrina looked at him.

"Do you know who hired us?"

"I presume the Criminal Gangs. The Governor, or who we knew as a High-Level Official, wasn't perfect but he was harsh on the gangs,"

Katrina slowly nodded. Wishing for a drink about now.

The ice formed quicker around her skin.

The crackling fire behind them slowed.

"It was a gang, but we were hired by The Old One,"

Locke's eyes widened.

His breathing quickened.

"You did what! The Old One- seriously! He is the worse criminal in the galaxy. He will kill us. Wait, is that who chased us and bombed our shuttle?"

Katrina nodded.

"I'm sorry, Locke. Yes, he attacked us, and he is hunting us,"

Locke stormed off.

Katrina chased after him.

Her armoured boots against the marble echoed around the hangar.

"Locke, I'm sorry. We don't have time to argue. He's coming,"

Locke stopped dead in his tracks.

"How does he know?"

Katrina paused.

"It was no mistake the bomb went off when it did. The Old One knew we would have to make an emergency landing, and this ancient space fleet from the Ancient Human Imperium is the closest site,"

Locke laughed and shook his head.

"Oh, Katrina. We are screwed. We're done for. We really have hired ourselves out for the last time,"

Katrina smiled a little.

"You knew this would happen?" Locke inquired.

"Now, now Locke. There was always a chance and I planned the routes. I researched these ships, but the enviro-systems are failing. We don't have long before the systems fail, and the ship explodes.

"Oh,"

"But the Ancient Imperium made excellent communication networks that are probably still intact. If we can get a message out then maybe help can arrive,"

"What! Help. You want the Empire to help us,"

Suddenly, Katrina and Locke were thrown to the floor.

The entire ship shook.

In the void of space, the wreckage churned and swirled around.

Chunks of marble collapsed into the hangar.

The temperature dropped.

Katrina jumped up.

Fear gripped them.

A black portal closed in space.

Allowing a small pod to exit Slidespace.

"Get up. It's the Old One. He exited Slidespace. He must have jumped from a nearby system,"

Locke slowly got up.

His head pounded.

Instantly, they collapsed once more.

Katrina's face landed hard against the floor.

She felt the lumps and bumps press against her face.

A deafening smash echoed through the entire ship, as the pod crashed into it.

Jumping up, Locke's and Katrina's mouths dropped, their eyes widened and they both tensed.

In front of them stood the Old One. Ready to slaughter them both.

***

Staring into the cold hard black eyes of the Old One, Katrina felt sweat turn to ice on her face.

Fear's grip upon her tightened.

The coldness of her icy skin turned even colder as the gravity of the situation sunk in.

For she as well as Locke were in the presence of a serial killer and one of the most notorious gang leaders in the galaxy.

Focusing on the Old One in detail, Katrina saw his long drawn out features that created a well-aged yet ugly face with tanned skin.

Then she looked down to see his thick, dense black spiky armour. With several guns and sharp blades attached to his waist belt.

His mere presence created an aura of pure fear.

Slowly, Katrina, as well as Locke, could feel their Will and determination being chipped away.

Although Katrina's nose turned up at the horrific smell of freshly slaughtered animals. Then she noticed the dark red footprints the Old One left behind as he walked over to them.

Katrina and Locke rushed back.

They both reached for their pistols on the belts, but something stopped them.

A gentle hummed filled the air.

Along with a cold metallic taste forming on

her tongue.

Memories and rage flashed over Katrina's mind as she remembered a similar situation in a past mission.

Through sheer force of Will, Katrina whipped out her gun.

Immense physical pain flooded her body.

A small black device exploded on the Old One.

Locke was released from the mental prison.

He whipped out his gun.

Pride filled Katrina as she aimed her pistol at the Old One.

"Clever, you using a Micro-prison on us,"

The Old One was silent.

Instead, he rotated on his heels.

"Why are you hunting us?" Locke demanded.

The Old One's eyebrows rose, and his head cocked to the right.

Slowly, he opened his mouth to talk in a dirty yet well-spoken voice.

"Us? I must apologise little mortal. I have travelled all across the Human Empire, across millions of space stations and planets. Not to find you both but to find her,"

The Old One pointed at Katrina.

Katrina took a step back.

"Kat, why is he hunting you?" Locke demanded. "What aren't you telling me?"

"Locke, the Old One is not just a criminal. He is..." Katrina began.

"You can say it," The Old One suggested.

"He's one of the most senior politicians in the Empire. He's the Emperor's Left Hand,"

The Old One beamed.

Locke's face spun.

Becoming a blur of confusion, fear, and outrage.

Locke stared at the Old One.

"I must apologise once again,"

"Why? How?"

Locke's mind spun.

Katrina tightened her fingers around the trigger of her pistol.

"This Old One pretends to support the Emperor, but in reality, he seeks to destroy him and replace him to become a new Emperor,"

Locke's face changed to utter horror.

As soon as his face had changed. It returned to its normal composed state.

Locke fixed his gun on the Old One's eyes.

"I may not love the Emperor for forcing billions of my friends to leave our Homeworld and be slaughtered on some unpronounceable battlefield. But I am loyal to the Throne!"

Immediately, they both fire their guns.

Their bullets screamed through the air.

Until they merely floated there.

Suddenly, the Old One flicked out his hands.

Unleashing a storm of electrical energy.

Katrina and Locke flew back.

Slamming into the hangar wall behind them.

Pain flooded violently through them.

Their worlds spun.

Their bodies ached.

Their ears rang.

Their vision cleared. Allowing them to see the Old One storm over.

His hands crackling with energy.
They fired again.
The Old One zapped their bullets away.
"Run!" Katrina ordered.
Immediately, they both surged forwards.
Charging towards a large metal door to their right.
They heard the constant crackling of energy behind them.
Katrina felt the heat of the energy behind her.
"Keep running!" she ordered.
Still the zapping energy chased them.
Running through the corridor, Katrina felt the coldness decreasing a little.
Her armoured feet on the warm white floors echoed around them.
Her skin turned wet as the ice melted.
"The ship's reactivating!" Locke reported.
A light exploded next to Katrina.
Sending glass shards into her face.
She didn't stop.
She kept running.
Blood dripped down her face.
They turned a corner.
Then another.
Then another.
Just ahead there were a series of doors, Katrina grabbed Locke and tackled him into one.
Immediately, she sealed the door.
Panting for air, they both kneeled on the hard-rough floor.
After a few moments of rapid panting, she crawled over to Locke. Trying to be silent but her metal armour made a small scraping sound across the

floor.

"Do you think he's gone?" Locke whispered.

Katrina shook her head and pointed over to a small pile of ancient technology from the age of the Ancient Imperium.

Crawling over to it, Locke passed her a small female necklace.

She smiled and thanked him. Knowing she could get a few thousand credits from a museum.

Carefully, looking through the pile of old tech, Katrina almost cried when she discovered a small tablet.

Running her fingers over its smooth screen, it hummed to life.

"What's that?" Locke questioned.

"This was known as a dataslate. More importantly, this is a dataslate that's wired into the ship's mainframe. I can scan the ship and send a distress call with this,"

Locke still wasn't sure if calling for aid from the Empire was a good idea.

"It might take the Empire years or even a decade to get names out to the entire Empire. But the police in local systems will know about us,"

Katrina ignored him.

"Got it. I can send power to the communication system for aid. We can escape!"

Locke shook his head.

"Even if our message gets sent. It will be years before the Empire can travel here,"

Katrina paused.

Sniffing the air rapidly.

"Do you smell that?"

Suddenly, immense columns of sparks shot

out from the door.

Katrina screamed: "He's trying to cut through the door!"

***

Sparks rapidly poured out of the thick metal door.

Slowly, the sparks started to move up the door frame.

Katrina frowned as she felt the immense burning sparks land on her leg armour.

Rage, wraith and pain flooded through her mind as she struggled to think.

Her mind was a haze of confusion.

Once again, her breath was rapid.

Sweat poured off her body.

Fear gripped her.

With one deep breath, she calmed herself.

However, a single memory flashed across her mind.

The memory of how she became a mercenary.

She shook her head as the memories of bombs exploding up her friends, their blood covering her face and fiery sparks of the alien weapons flooded her mind.

"We need a new plan!" Katrina ordered.

"Kat, we need to escape now! Is there a zoomer about?"

"We don't have time for your slang,"

"Um, shuttle,"

Katrina and Locke ran backwards as a massive torrent of sparks jetted out of the frame.

The cut rapidly continued.

Cold air rushed in from the corridor.

Katrina tapped hard on the dataslate.

Swiping this and that.

Her face lit up.

"Yes, a few corridors down there's a lift. It takes you directly down to the hangar and there are about a hundred fighters,"

Red hot metal leaked onto the floor. Releasing the foul burning smell of rubber and sulphur.

The cold breeze of the corridor kept brushing Katrina's skin.

"Can you fly an Imperial Fighter?" Locke questioned.

Katrina paused.

"Maybe,"

"Maybe?"

The sparks stopped.

Katrina whipped out her gun.

Locke did the same.

Silence.

Katrina's breath formed solid ice in front of her.

Smashing onto the ground.

The door slammed onto the floor.

Katrina and Locke fired.

A cloud of black smoke engulfed the entrance.

The flashes of gunfire lit up their faces.

Nothing.

The smoke cleared.

No one was there.

Katrina and Locke stopped firing.

Suddenly, the Old One surged forward.

Zapping Locke.

Katrina charged towards him.

Firing her pistol.

The Old One left hooked her.

Katrina's blood-spattered up the wall.

Charging forward, she slammed her fists into the Old One.

His head snapped back.

Locke grabbed his gun.

He fired.

The shots roared through the air.

Landing into the Old One's chest.

No blood poured out.

Flickering his hand, the Old One zapped Katrina and Locke. Sending them back into the wall.

Energy flooded their bodies.

Bones cracked.

Muscles tensed.

Their backs pressed against the freezing glass window.

A small cracking sound started behind her.

The Old One frowned.

Katrina stared at him.

Her skin turned damp from fresh cold sweat.

Her mouth turned dry.

Locke stared at Katrina.

She did the same.

His eyes were wide, their breathing slow and there was something his eyes.

They did not show fear.

They did not show rage.

They showed- acceptance.

Locke simply nodded to her.

Katrina's stomach flipped.

Using her sheer force of Will, Katrina managed to stop herself from vomiting.

The sound of cracking glass got louder and

quicker.

Memories of seeing frozen dead bodies pulled from the void made her skin turn ghostly white.

"Old One! Stop!" Katrina commanded.

The zapping decreased.

"I may want peace. I may want to die, but I will die on my own terms," Katrina shouted.

Getting her breathing under control, her muscles relaxed.

The Old One stopped. His eyebrows rose and a smile formed across his thin blood-red lips.

"My apologies, Katrina. You are mistaken. You will die,"

"No, I won't,"

Suddenly, she surged forward.

Kicking the Old One to the ground.

Running towards the door.

The Old One jumped up. Spun around, and raced after her.

Locke whipped out a dagger and stabbed the glass.

It cracked.

Katrina dashed out the door.

The Old One's eyes narrowed.

Locke slammed the dagger back down on the glass.

It shattered.

The cold void flooded into the chamber.

An immense vacuumed screamed overhead.

Katrina covered her ears.

Taking a deep breath, she poked her head around the door.

Only to see Locke smile at her as frost covered his body and he was thrown out into the void of space.

The Old One started to fall forward.

Katrina took out her dataslate and slammed the emergency door down.

Trapping the Old One in the chamber.

Afterwards, Katrina fell against the emergency door.

If bare skin touched it, then it would have stuck.

A gentle coldness touched her skin under her thick armour.

She almost gasped for air as the ship hummed to life correcting its enviro-systems.

Tears welled up in her eyes as she replayed the memory of Locke's body being thrown into the void again and again.

"You always were faithful and loyal," she muttered.

Tears flooded down her face. Becoming crystalised when it touched her armour.

After a few precious moments of grieving, she forced herself up and paced towards the hangar.

She jumped.

Immense banging came from the chamber door.

Thunderous knocks echoed in the corridor.

Then the ear-splitting sound of ripping metal caused Katrina's ears to bleed.

"I will not apologise for that. I'm going to rip your heart out and feed it to you!" the Old One roared.

***

Katrina's eyes narrowed.

Rage built within her.

"How the hell did he live?" Kat muttered.

With her fate closing in around her, she refused to let fear grip her.

She needed to focus.

What did she have?

Closing her eyes, she heard immense chunks of metal being ripped out of the door.

The Old Ones was slowly yet purposefully escaping.

The grand howling void was stopped.

It was stopped!

Opening her eyes, Katrina scanned the dataslate.

She hit herself on the forehead.

"Emperor damn these Imperials. When I shut the emergency door, I don't want to shut the damn emergency window as well!"

Closing her eyes once more, she blocked out the sounds around her.

A gentle draft flowed through the corridor. Gentling stroking her cheeks with an icy touch.

She went to gasp with inspiration, but a foul artificial taste forced her to cough.

Kat almost smiled at the memory of the taste accompanying her on all her space travels across the Human Empire.

Followed by an intense wave of sadness washing over her as she remembered the space battles and the dead friends. She had left behind.

The tearing of the doors stopped.

Snapping open her eyes, she saw the Old One climb out of the chamber.

He grinned.

Her body instantly tensed.

The Old One slowly started to stalk her down the corridor.

Katrina's mind wanted to freeze.

Her muscles wanted to fight.

Katrina ran.

The Old One charged after her.

Icy air whipped around her.

Her feet boomed on the white metal floor.

Her mouth became dry with fear.

Katrina swung around corners as she ran.

Ducking under broken cables.

Bullets ricocheted around her.

Metal shards flew towards her.

Katrina felt the warmth of the bullets against her arms.

Flickering up her hand, she threw the dataslate behind her.

It whirled through the air.

Barely missing the Old One.

Ahead she could see the lift.

"Katrina!" the Old One screamed.

A tear formed in Kat's eye.

Two doors were open nearby.

She missed the first one.

Whipping out her gun, she fired into the ceiling.

Electrical cables poured out behind her.

The Old One stopped in his tracks.

Katrina dived into the second door.

She pressed the holographic door controls, but the door only shut.

It didn't have a lock on it.

She spat at the door controls.

Walking over a giant sterile white wall,

Katrina lent against it.

Catching her breath.

She rested her hands against the wall only to feel a fleshy wet liquid coat them.

Looking back down, she saw a bucket of body parts.

"What?" Katrina asked.

She stood up straight and looked around the chamber.

To see the pile of medical supplies and medical body parts used in organ transplants.

Turning to her right, she saw the medical freezer in the room had been opened. Causing the body parts to fall out onto the floor.

After wiping her hand clean, Katrina wondered over to the freezer.

A pleasantly refreshing warmth came from the freezer.

She rubbed her hands together.

Finally, relieved to not see her breath turn to columns of vapour.

Peeking into the freezer, Katrina saw a few bottles of sealed medical-grade water.

She didn't hesitate.

She grabbed a bottle and poured it down her throat.

In return, her throat opened lovingly. The water wetted her mouth and refreshed her.

Although, a terrible chemical taste was left in her mouth.

Stepping forward, her ankle almost twisted on something.

Katrina knelt down and picked up a small pen-like object.

"Wow, cool. A Wound-Sealer,"

She clicked the top and a small laser beam shot out.

Her eyes widened.

Outside, Katrina heard movement.

Heavy footsteps stormed towards the door.

Surging forward, she dragged the pile of water bottles to the middle of the Freezer.

The footsteps got louder.

Katrina dashed out of the freezer.

Checked the control panels.

Turned on the Freezer.

Violent hums thundered through the room.

Then silence.

Katrina shivered.

Her breath became a thick column of vapour.

The footsteps stopped.

Katrina dashed into the corner by the door.

The door exploded open.

Katrina grabbed the Old One.

Throwing him into the freezer.

She clicked the pen.

A laser beam shot out.

Hit the freezer.

Causing it to become engulfed in flames.

Kat clicked the pen again.

A laser beam hit the water bottles.

They exploded.

Engulfing the Old One in flames.

He screamed.

Katrina dashed out the room.

The Old One's screams echoed along the corridor.

"Thank you, Locke," Kat whispered.

A memory of him explaining the reaction between a laser beam, the weird medical plastic and the chemicals in the water flashing across her mind.

Arriving at the lift, she opened it.

Dived in.

Ordered the lift to go down to the hangar.

The lift doors slammed shut and she descended.

Katrina fell to the floor in delight.

She had finally killed the Old One and escaped.

"I'm free," she whispered.

Her muscles relaxed and her fingers traced along the smooth shiny flooring of the lift.

It pulsed at her touch.

Sending bright colourful light into the lift.

She busted out laughing as her chest became lighter.

No longer did she have to constantly watch her back.

The Old One was dead.

Then she paused.

Sadness filled her as she remembered Locke.

She had never told him why the Old One was hunting her.

"I never should have agreed to kill him for the Old One,"

A few tears poured out from her eyes.

"I'm sorry, Locke. I didn't know this would happen. I thought... I thought I could do the Governor business then the Old One would agree to let you live. Oh, why did I agree to let him kill you,"

The lift began to slow.

Katrina stood up.

Brushing the strange alien dust off her armour, glad she had a medical implant to protect her from the disease.

Walking over to the door, she smiled. Thinking about the glorious sight of the Imperial fighters.

Her heart sang in delight as she remembered the glorious memories of flying previous Imperial fighters during special op training.

The lift stopped.

Katrina smiled.

The doors opened.

A hand shot out.

Grabbing her by the throat.

Katrina's vision blurred.

Thick nails dug into her skin.

Looking down the hand, she saw the Old One.

***

The Old One's long scaly fingers clawed their way into Katrina's flesh.

Her eyes flashed with rage as the long talons pressed into her smooth white flesh. As well as small droplets of bright red blood started to ooze out of the wound.

'This is no time to panic' Katrina thought using her Will to make her obey.

Instead her eyes narrowed on her attacker.

His fingers, hand and arm were covered in thick layers of red bluish scales.

They grated hard against her skin.

Katrina wanted to scream so badly.

Looking past the menacing talons clawing their way through her skin. Katrina saw the Old

One's long dark cloak covering his scaly arm.

Attached to an extremely dark black cloak.

However, whilst the cloak outlined a thick muscular body beneath the cloak. Something hummed and vibrated along his body. Sending gentle vibrations into Katrina's neck.

She paused.

Listening to the air, Kat heard a slight ringing coming from the Old One.

Through her searing pain, she forced her mind to focus on those vibrations. Running through her memory to try and place the familiar feelings.

The Old One squeezed a little harder.

Staring into the Old One's eyes, Kat only saw delight at her suffering.

Then the memory hit her, she knew exactly how the Old One had been surviving this entire time.

She opened her mouth then she closed it once more.

If she told the Old One what she knew she was dead.

Katrina's eyes turned to focus on the hangar itself with the sniffs of artificial and poorly recycled air invading her nose.

Focusing on the hangar, Katrina saw a massive endless grey chamber that was hundreds of kilometres tall but thousands of kilometres wide.

Her skin was freezing to the touch as the chamber was nothing more than a frozen wasteland after decades without heating.

On the smooth white ceiling, a small heating unit tried to change that fact, but caught on fire.

Ripping her fingernails into the scales, Katrina tried to weaken the Old One's grip.

Nothing happened.

The Old One banged her head into the wall.

Only pain radiated from the wound.

Her hair turned red.

Nonetheless, Katrina still smiled a little.

The headbanging had allowed her to move her head just a little.

She smiled once more.

Whilst the rest of the hangar was empty of the Imperial fighters, just a few metre metres from her laid an Imperial Shuttle.

The craft's long angelic white wings shone brightly in the artificial light of the hangar.

While it's white hawk-like body shone in the starlight that poured into the hangar via the massive semi-shielded doorway into the hangar.

The Old One jerked Katrina.

Walking over to the doorway in the hangar.

He stormed over there.

Holding Kat by the throat firmly.

She gasped for air.

The Old One stopped.

Kat's body jerked forward.

Her vision cleared.

Bright stars and the endless void filled her vision.

The Old One squeezed hard.

His talons ripped into her flesh.

Blood poured out.

Katrina screamed.

He squeezed harder.

Then she choked, gasped, and gagged.

The Old One chuckled.

"Teleporter!" Katrina managed.

His grip lightened on her neck.

"What about my teleporter?"

Katrina's head went light with dizziness.

"That's how you've been hunting us and surviving!"

He nodded with a grin.

The Old One's arm tensed.

Katrina needed to act.

Her heart raced.

Her brain spun.

"Why did you need Locke dead?"

The Old One licked his lips.

"The Emperor had plans for you both. He wanted you to be more than mercenaries. He wanted you to be… I don't know. I wouldn't let you two risk my operations. You two are a team. If he dies, you are far from a threat to me,"

Rage built inside Katrina.

"You murdered my friend!"

"Oh well,"

Katrina whacked him across the face.

She whipped out her nail.

Forcing it into his right black eye.

He roared in agony.

The Old One released her.

She ran back.

An intense jolt of energy burned her leg.

She reached for her gun.

It wasn't on her belt.

Katrina looked up.

The Old One aimed her own gun at her head.

Searing pain blinded her senses.

Running her fingers over the burned, smouldering remains of her leg armour. She noticed her armour and flesh were one.

She pressed hard against her leg.

Katrina didn't feel a thing.

Kicking her leg, it moved as if was something other than her own body.

Horror filled her.

Her stomach churned.

"You cost me my leg!" she boomed.

The Old One cocked the barrel.

In utter defiance, Katrina forced herself to drag her body across the floor.

Her skin felt every single bump and lump in the hard-white floor.

Afterwards, when she reached the Old One. He smiled.

She grabbed onto his cloak.

Dragging herself up him.

Looking him in the eye, Katrina demanded: "If I'm... going to die. Let me see a teleporter,"

He shook his head.

Whacking him around the face.

Katrina ripped open his cloak.

Grabbing the little blue disc teleporter.

Pushed herself away.

Knocking herself to the floor.

The Old One charged towards her.

Katrina rapidly pressed a few buttons.

Flicked a switch.

The Old One snatched it from her hands.

His eyes widened.

His face drained in colour.

Blue columns of smoke engulfed him.

The Old One tried to deactivate the teleporter, but it was too late.

The blue smoke engulfed him.

His body dematerialised.

A patch of blue smoke materialised in the endless black void of space.

The Old One appeared.

His mouth opened. Trying to scream as the vacuum of space turned his body to ice.

A few seconds later, his frozen body hit the side of the ship. Shattering it.

Rolling herself over, Katrina dragged herself over to the Imperial shuttle.

She banged on the side. Creating an immense echoing sound throughout the hangar.

The large wiry ramp lowered to the floor with a thump.

Slowly, Katrina dragged herself up the ramp.

The wires that formed the ramp run over her body. Tickling her.

A bleach smell assaulted her nostrils as fresh air entered the shuttle for the first time in centuries.

After climbing onto the shuttle, she barely saw the sterile white box-like cockpit as the realm of sleep took her.

Just before her eyes closed, Katrina commanded: "Take me to Earth,"

As her eyelids slammed shut, she heard the shuttle hum to life, the engines roared and she felt the shuttle zoom out of the hangar.

https://www.subscribepage.com/garrosignup

https://www.subscribepage.com/wintersignup

GET YOUR FREE AND EXCLUSIVE SHORT STORY NOW! LEARN ABOUT NEMESIO'S PAST!

https://www.subscribepage.com/fireheart

Thank you for reading.

I hoped you enjoyed it.

If you want a FREE book and keep up to date about new books and project. Then please sign up for my newsletter at www.connorwhiteley.net/

Have a great day.

About the author:

Connor Whiteley is the author of over 30 books in the sci-fi fantasy, nonfiction psychology and books for writer's genre and he is a Human Branding Speaker and Consultant.

He is a passionate warhammer 40,000 reader, psychology student and author.

Who narrates his own audiobooks and he hosts The Psychology World Podcast.

All whilst studying Psychology at the University of Kent, England.

Also, he was a former Explorer Scout where he gave a speech to the Maltese President in August 2018 and he attended Prince Charles' 70th Birthday Party at Buckingham Palace in May 2018.

Plus, he is a self-confessed coffee lover!

OTHER SHORT STORIES BY CONNOR WHITELEY

Blade of The Emperor

Arbiter's Truth

The Bloodied Rose

Asmodia's Wrath

Heart of A Killer

Emissary of Blood

Computation of Battle

Old One's Wrath

Other books by Connor Whiteley:

The Fireheart Fantasy Series

Heart of Fire

Heart of Lies

More Coming Soon!

The Garro Series- Fantasy/Sci-fi

GARRO: GALAXY'S END

GARRO: RISE OF THE ORDER

GARRO: END TIMES

GARRO: SHORT STORIES

GARRO: COLLECTION

GARRO: HERESY

GARRO: FAITHLESS

GARRO: DESTROYER OF WORLDS

GARRO: COLLECTIONS BOOK 4-6

GARRO: MISTRESS OF BLOOD

GARRO: BEACON OF HOPE

GARRO: END OF DAYS

<u>Winter Series- Fantasy Trilogy Books</u>

WINTER'S COMING

WINTER'S HUNT

WINTER'S REVENGE

WINTER'S DISSENSION

<u>Miscellaneous:</u>

THE ANGEL OF RETURN

THE ANGEL OF FREEDOM

www.ingramcontent.com/pod-product-compliance
Lightning Source LLC
LaVergne TN
LVHW011901060526
838200LV00054B/4460